What My Daddy Loves

RAISSA FIGUEROA

CLARION BOOKS
An Imprint of HarperCollinsPublishers

Clarion Books is an imprint of HarperCollins Publishers.

What My Daddy Loves

Copyright © 2023 by Raissa Figueroa

All rights reserved. Manufactured in Italy. No part of this book may be used or reproduced in any manner whatsoever without written permission except in the case of brief quotations embodied in critical articles and reviews. For information address HarperCollins Children's Books, a division of HarperCollins Publishers, 195 Broadway, New York, NY 10007.

www.harpercollinschildrens.com

ISBN 978-0-35-858877-1

The artist used Procreate on the iPad Pro to create the digital illustrations for this book.

Typography by Celeste Knudsen

23 24 25 26 27 RTLO 10 9 8 7 6 5 4 3 2 1

First Edition

To my dad. To all dads.
What a wonderful gift you've been given.

My daddy loves
starting the day with me.

My daddy loves
eating with me.

My daddy loves
playing with me.

My daddy loves
discovering with me.

My daddy loves
trying new things with me.

My daddy loves studying with me.

My daddy loves
building with me.

My daddy loves exploring with me.

My daddy loves
sitting with me.

My daddy loves
creating with me.

My daddy loves
fixing things with me.

My daddy loves
growing with me.

My daddy loves dreaming with me.

I love my daddy.

And I know that what
my daddy loves most of all . . .